Iblis

RETOLD BY

Shulamith Levey Oppenheim

ILLUSTRATED BY

Ed Young

Harcourt Brace & Company

SAN DIEGO   NEW YORK   LONDON

Requests for permission to make copies of any part
of the work should be mailed to: Permissions
Department, Harcourt Brace & Company,
8th Floor, Orlando, Florida 32887.

Library of Congress Cataloging-in-Publication Data
Oppenheim, Shulamith Levey.
Iblis: an Islamic tale/by Shulamith Oppenheim;
illustrated by Ed Young.—1st ed.
p.   cm.
Summary: An Islamic version of the story of Adam
and Eve and the fall from Paradise.
ISBN 0-15-238016-7
1. Islamic stories—Juvenile literature. [1. Islamic stories.
2. Adam (Biblical figure). 3. Eve (Biblical figure).]
I. Young, Ed, ill. II. Title.
BP88.066I25   1994
297'.43—dc20   92-15060

First edition
A B C D E

Printed in Singapore

The illustrations in this book were done in pastel and
watercolor on Canson paper.
The display type was hand lettered by Judythe Sieck,
San Diego,California.
The text type was set in Deepdene by Harcourt Brace
& Company, Photocomposition Center, San Diego,
California.
Color separations were made by Bright Arts, Ltd.,
Singapore.
Printed and bound by Tien Wah Press, Singapore
Production supervision by Warren Wallerstein and
David Hough
Designed by Michael Farmer

For Robert Haddad

—S.L.O.

To Andrew Tseng
for his unassuming multitalents,
enduring resilience, and his wisdom

—E.Y.

AUTHOR'S NOTE

The story in this book has been told for thousands of years, and like Iblis (pronounced e-blees), it has taken many forms.

The best-known form appears in the Bible and the First Book of Moses and is thought by some scholars to date back to the ninth century B.C. It is both a creation story, explaining the beginnings of humankind and our troubles, and a cautionary tale, showing the dangers of disobeying God's orders. In most versions, a serpent represents the devil, or evil, who tempts Eve, the first woman on earth, to eat forbidden food (sometimes an apple or a pomegranate). In the Koran, the sacred book of Islam, Adam and his wife dwell in Paradise until Satan brings about their banishment.

The Islamic version from which this story is retold can be found in the work of Jarir at-Tabari, a famous Islamic scholar who was a religious authority and historian. Born about 839 A.D. in Amul, a city near the southern shore of the Caspian Sea, he traveled throughout the Islamic world as a young man and finally settled in Baghdad, in what is now Iraq. He acquired material for his history of the world from oral storytelling and literary sources, as well as from the Koran.

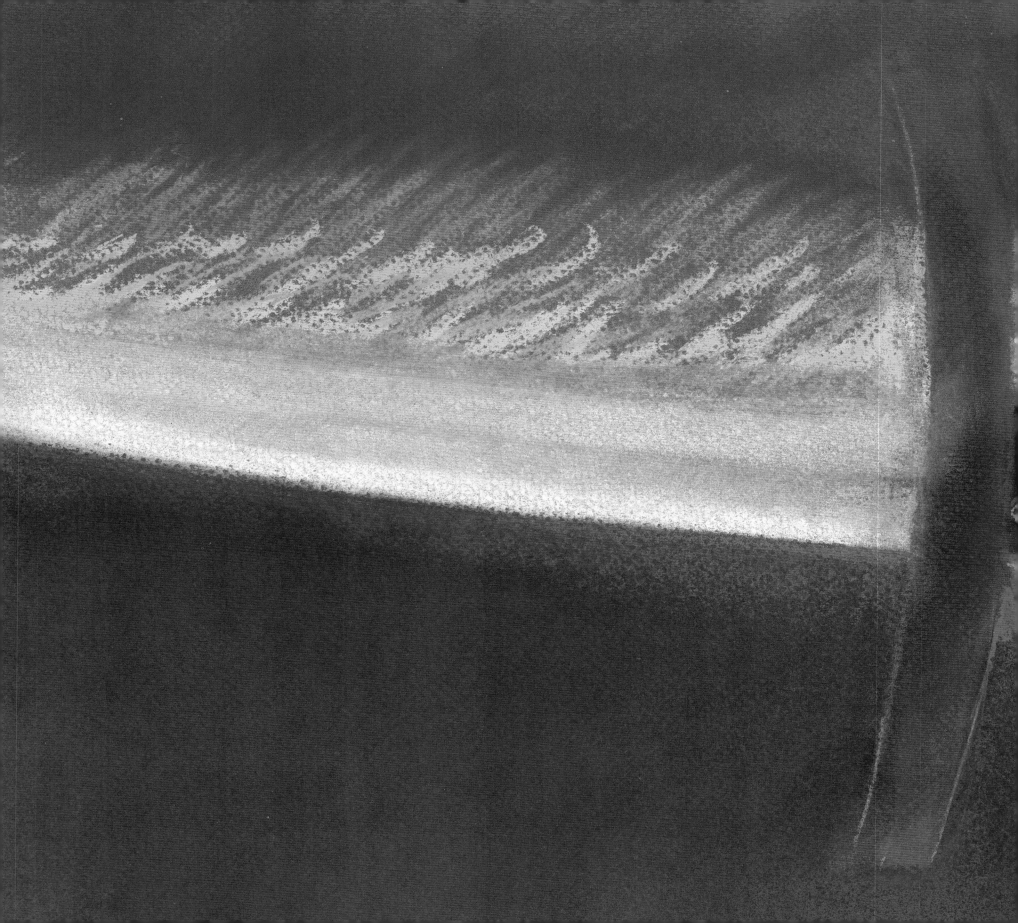

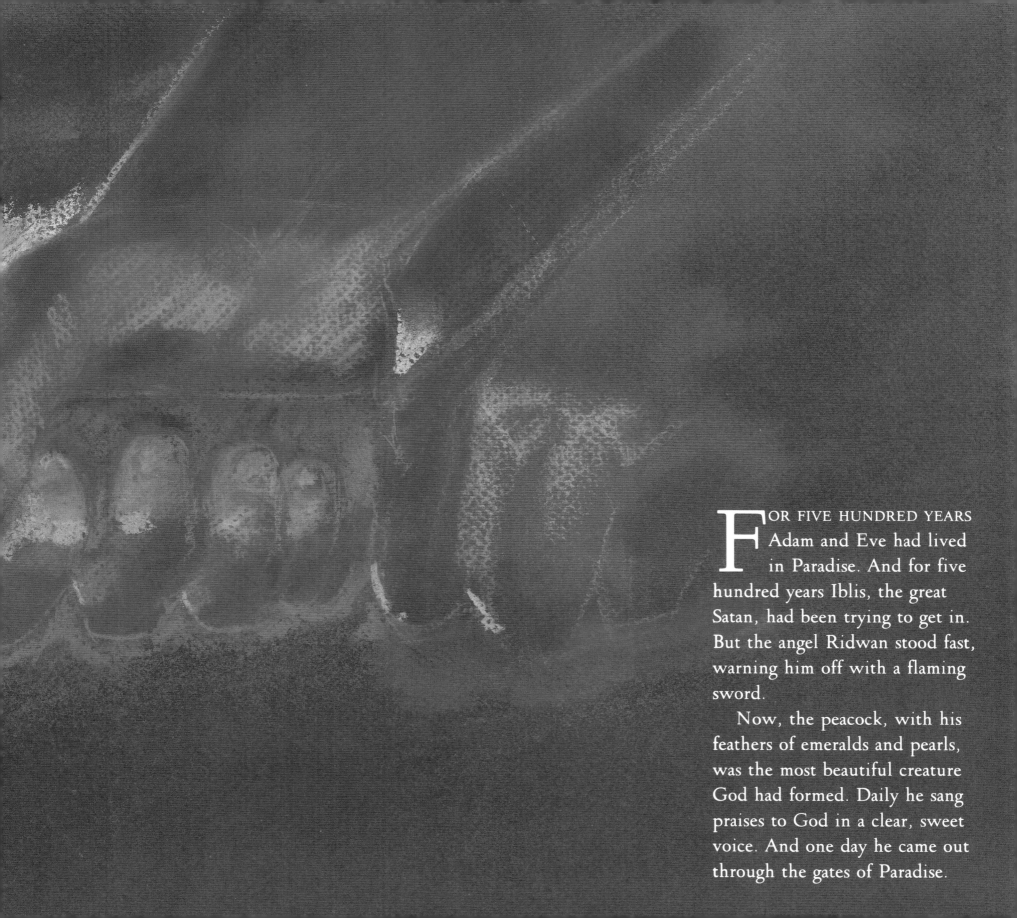

FOR FIVE HUNDRED YEARS Adam and Eve had lived in Paradise. And for five hundred years Iblis, the great Satan, had been trying to get in. But the angel Ridwan stood fast, warning him off with a flaming sword.

Now, the peacock, with his feathers of emeralds and pearls, was the most beautiful creature God had formed. Daily he sang praises to God in a clear, sweet voice. And one day he came out through the gates of Paradise.

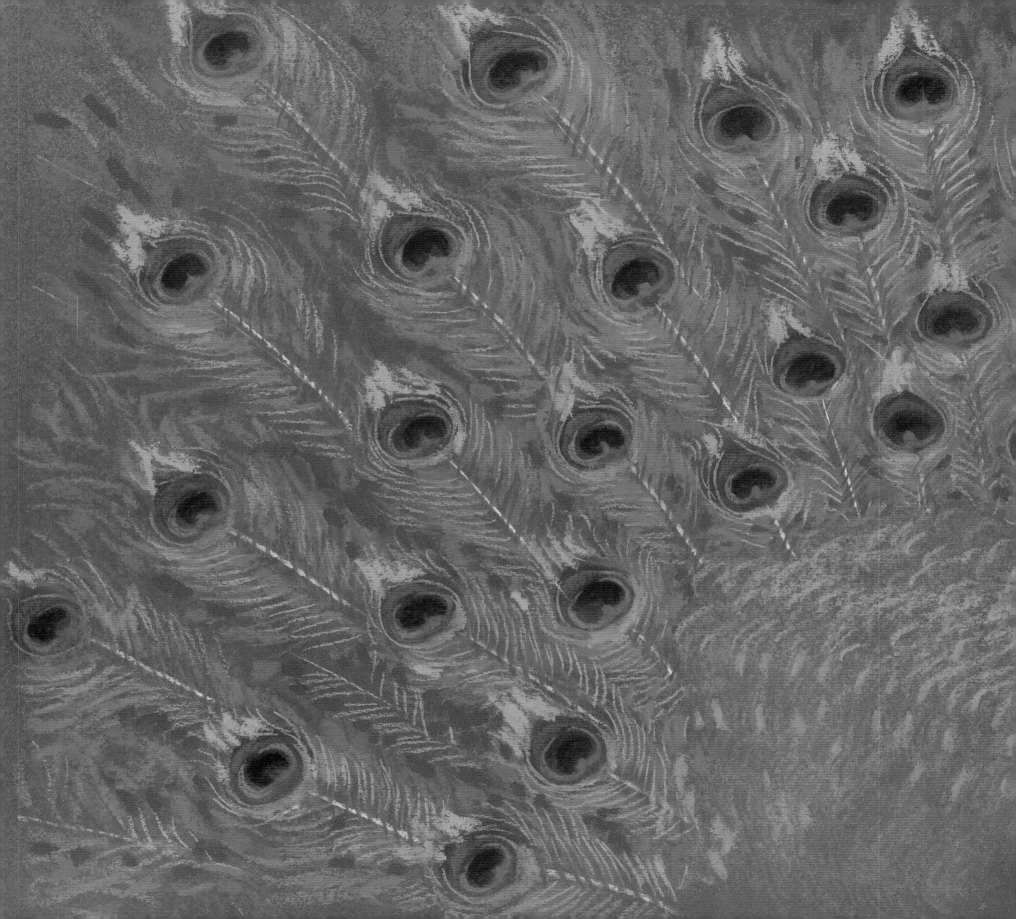

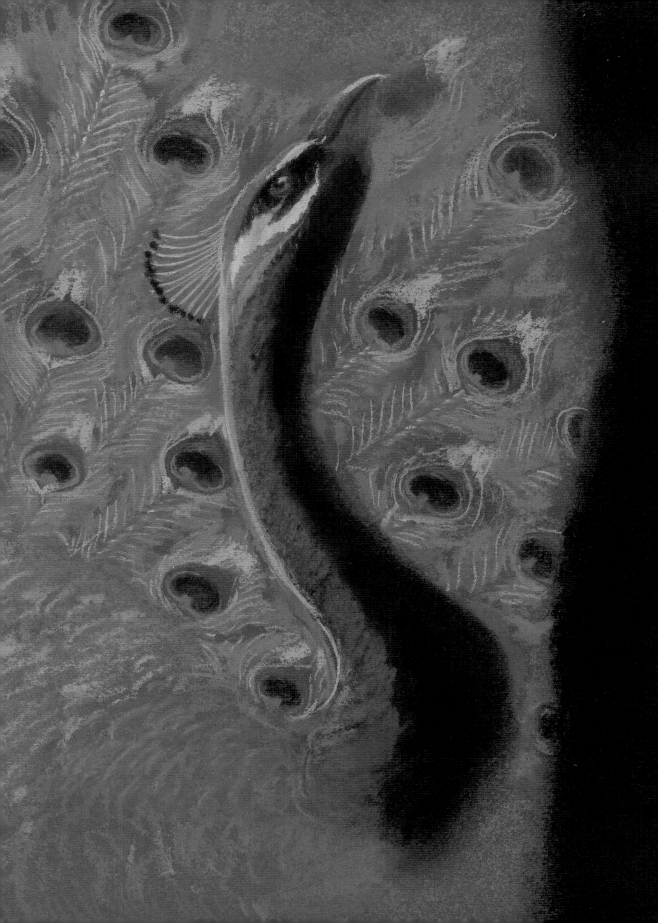

Aha! thought Iblis, this bird will surely listen to flattery, for there is no doubt he is vain.

Sidling up to the peacock, Iblis spoke in his most beguiling manner. "Most beautiful of birds, do you live within the gates of Paradise?"

The peacock spread his tail to full magnificence. "I do. But why do you look from side to side with fear and trembling? Who are you?"

"I?" Iblis struggled for a more casual tone. "I belong to the angels who praise God day and night. I have slipped away that I might glimpse this Paradise that God has created. Will you hide me under your gorgeous feathers and show me the garden?"

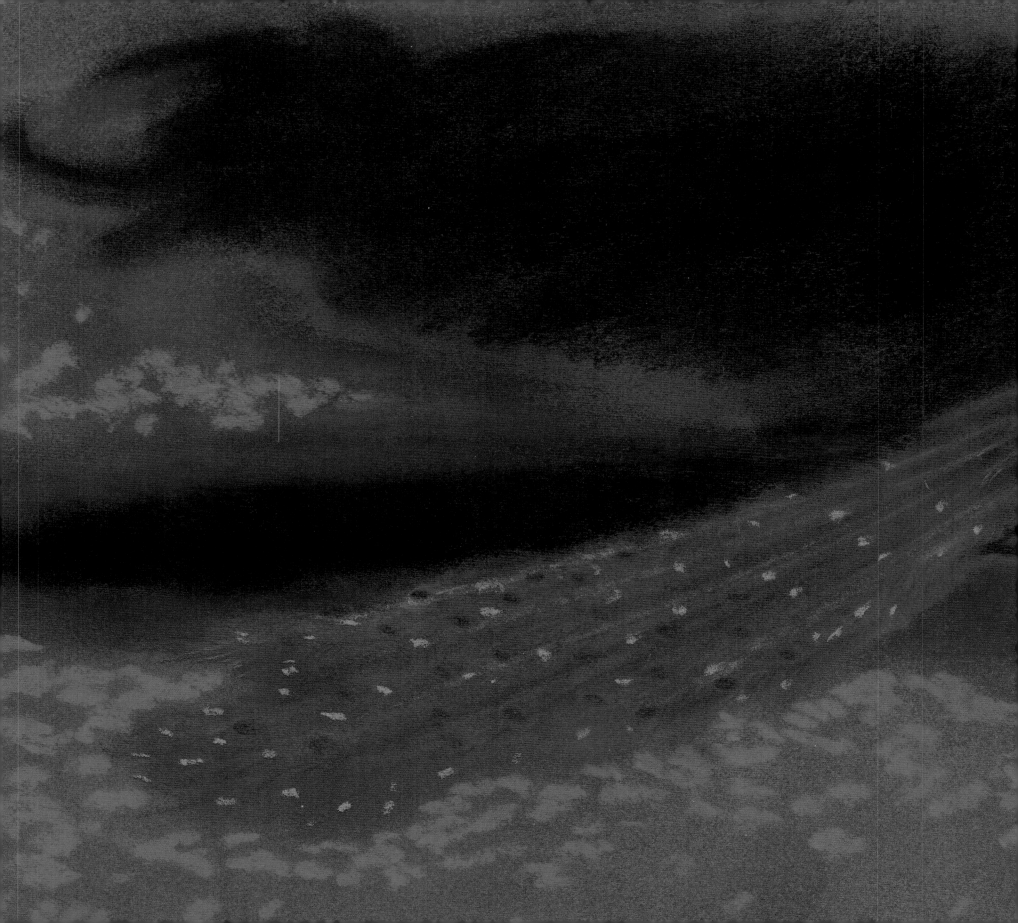

Immediately the peacock folded down his tail. "This I cannot do, for it would draw upon me God's disfavor."

The wicked angel put his mouth to the peacock's ear. "O revered creature, if you take me with you, I will teach you three words that will save you from illness, old age, and death."

Curious, the peacock turned to Iblis. "Are you telling me that all who dwell within must become ill, grow old, and die?"

"All," hissed Iblis. "All except those who know the three words."

"Are you telling me the truth?" the peacock asked.

"By God Almighty it is true."

The peacock could not believe that a living creature would swear a false oath by his Creator. But he knew Ridwan was a most vigilant watchman. So he promised Iblis that he would send out the serpent. "Even more than myself," the peacock told him, "this wise and beautiful creature will desire youth and health everlasting. She will know a way to take you into Paradise."

The serpent! She had been created a thousand years before man and was Eve's favorite companion. She had a head like emeralds and eyes like opals. As soon as she heard the story, the serpent exclaimed, "Never! Never shall I become infirm, grow old, and die! My face wrinkled, my eyes closed, my body dissolved into dust? Never! I shall risk Ridwan's search."

In the darkness of night the serpent glided out of Paradise and asked Iblis to tell her the three words.

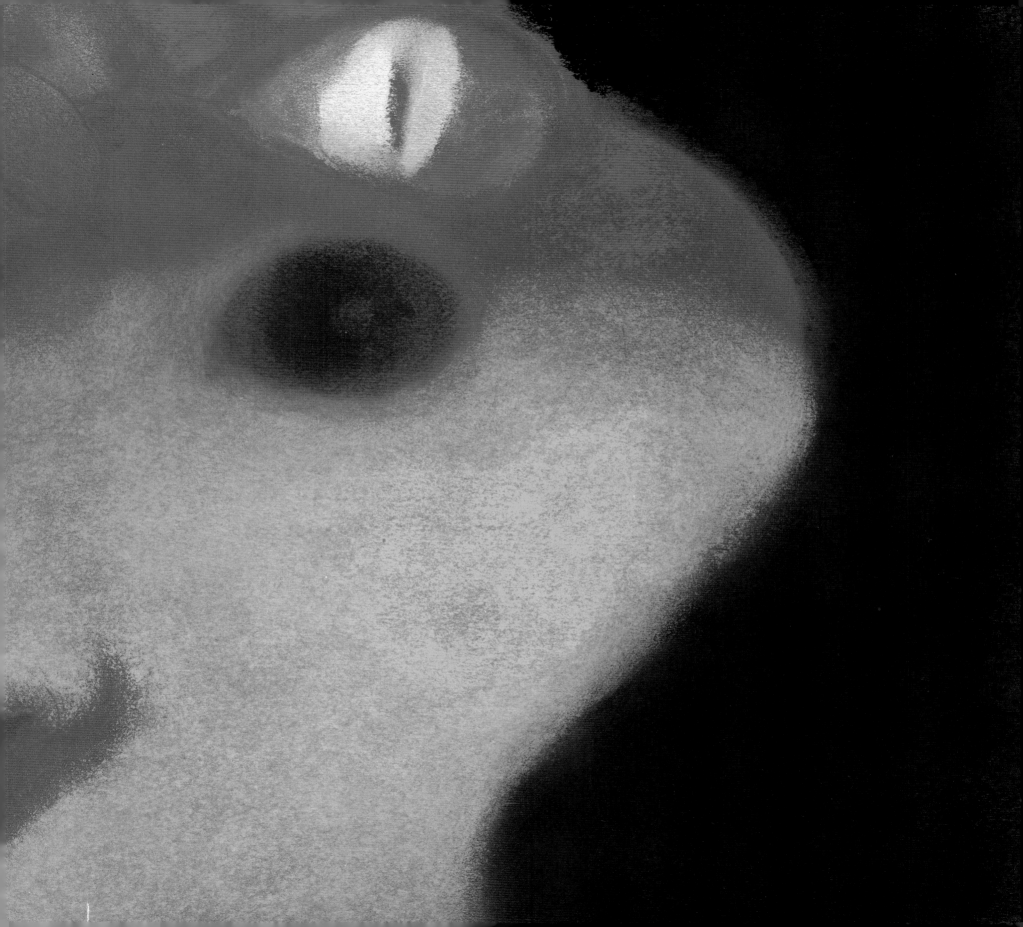

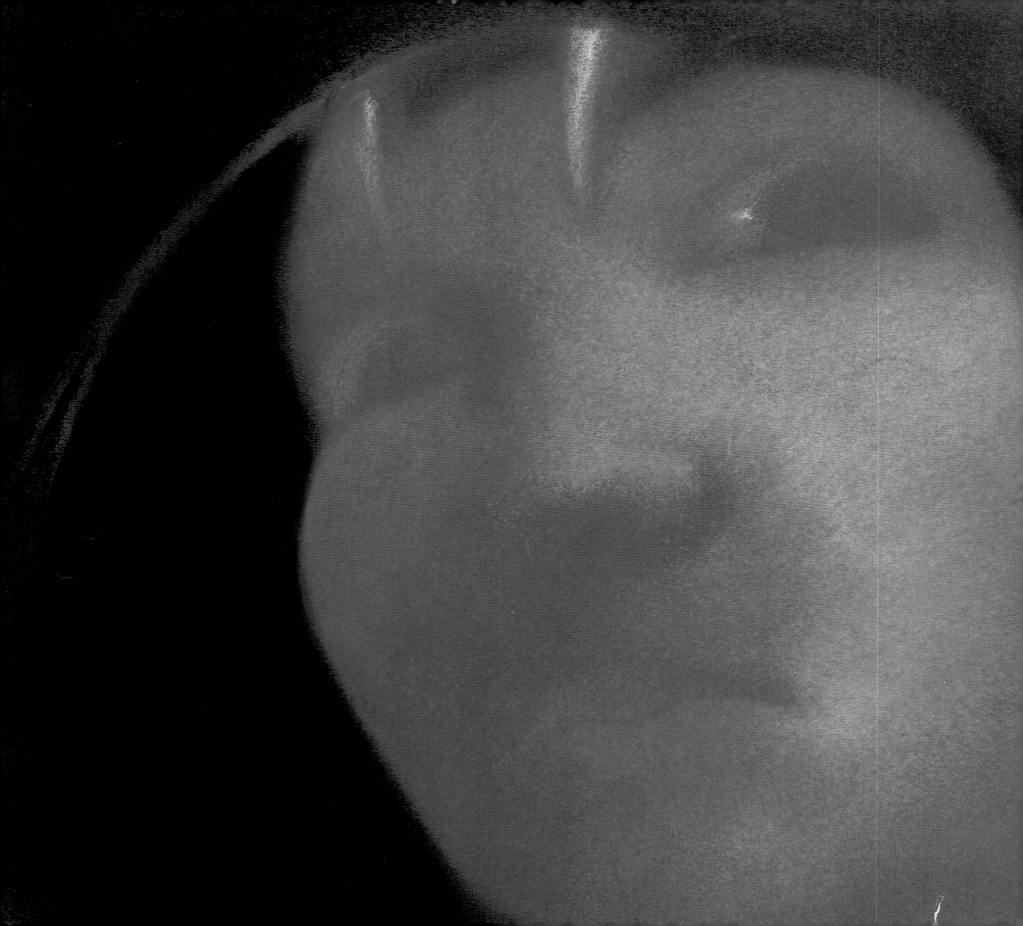

"First," commanded the crafty devil, "take me into Paradise unobserved."

Looking into the face of Iblis, the serpent, who had never known fear, shuddered at what she saw there.

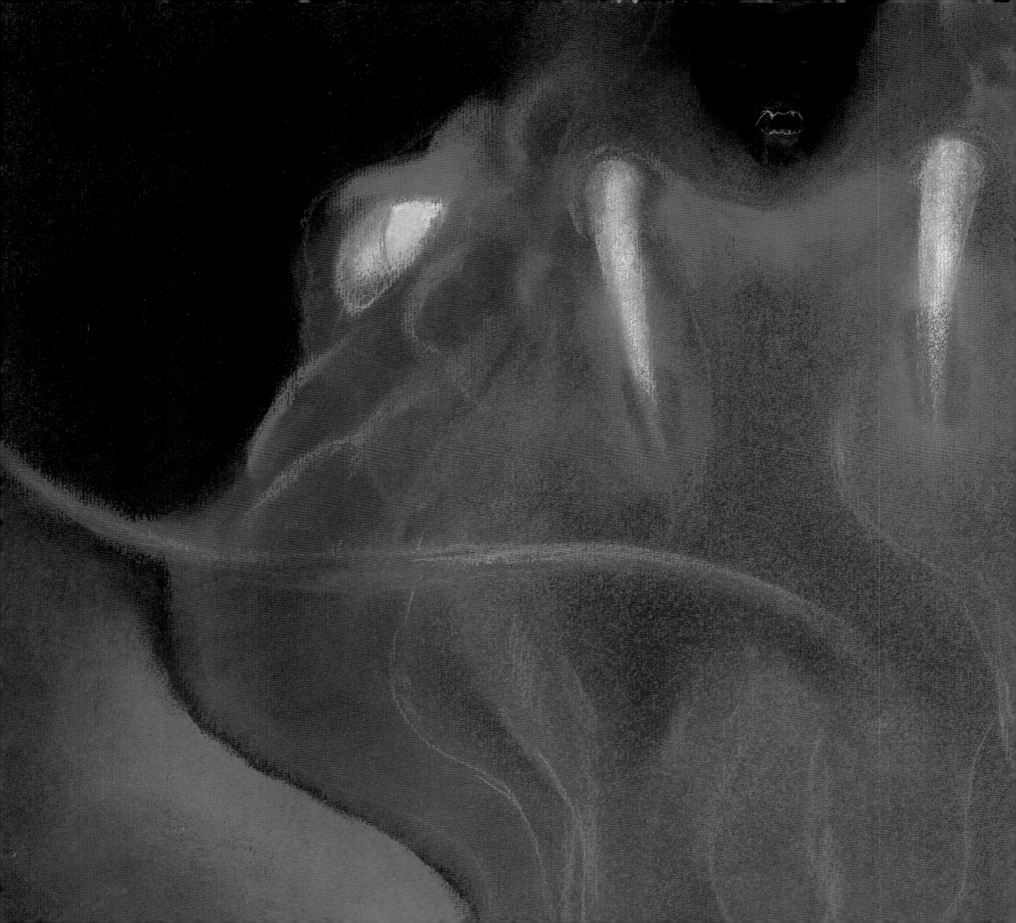

"How shall I do this?" Her voice trembled.

"I have given it much thought. I shall make myself so small that I can sit in the nick between your teeth," answered Iblis.

"How then will I be able to speak when Ridwan addresses me?"

The devil! Iblis had an answer for everything. "No need for fear, my beauty. I shall whisper holy names. Ridwan will keep silent."

Still uneasy, but craving to retain her youth and beauty, the serpent opened her mouth. Whereupon Iblis, shrinking to the size of a speck of dust, seated himself between her teeth, making them poisonous for eternity.

As Iblis predicted, Ridwan lowered his flaming sword as soon as he heard the holy names. Once inside Paradise, the serpent asked again for the three magic words. But Iblis announced that he first wished to speak to Eve. The serpent consented, driven on by her vanity.

Reaching the tent of Adam and Eve, Iblis uttered a great sigh. It was the first sigh heard in Paradise.

"O gentle friend, why are you troubled?" Eve knelt and caressed the serpent's head. But Iblis was not troubled. The sigh was envy, the first envy felt in Paradise.

"I am troubled for your future, my friend," the evil spirit answered.

"Dearest serpent, in this garden of God, have we not all that can be desired?"

"It would seem so. But are you not troubled that the noblest fruit of the garden is denied to you by God?"

Eve smiled and shook her head. "I am content. Only one fruit is forbidden."

Though Eve smiled, Iblis observed a shadow cross her face. He rejoiced and pushed on.

"But if you knew why it was forbidden, all the other fruit would mean nothing to you."

Eve stood up. Her hair shone in the morning sun, but her eyes were clouded. "Do *you* know why, my dearest friend?"

From his perch between the serpent's teeth, Iblis shivered with delight. "I do, and this is why I sigh. This fruit alone gives eternal youth and health."

Eve moved away from the serpent. "Why did you not tell me this before? And how do you know this?"

"An angel," he whispered. "An angel told me as I lay under the forbidden tree."

"I must see this angel!" Eve ran out of the tent to the tree in the middle of Paradise.

The serpent moved ahead of her. When Eve reached the tree, Iblis flew out of the serpent's mouth and stood before her. He was a perfect young man with wings like clouds—a wondrous being. Eve was dazzled.

"Who are you?" she asked.

"I am a man made into an angel," Iblis told her. Then he waited for the question sure to follow.

"And how did you become an angel?"

Iblis rejoiced. He pointed to the forbidden tree. "I became an angel by eating the fruit that God has denied us. I was near death, ill and infirm. I ate and lo, you see me a thousand years later."

"Do you speak the truth?" Eve was frightened by the devil's words.

"I swear by God who created me."

Like the peacock, Eve could
not believe that anyone would
swear falsely on the name of the
Creator. And so she broke a
branch from the wheat tree.

Now, in those days, wheat
grew the size of small trees. The
leaves were emeralds. The grains
were white as snow and sweet as
honey. Eve ate one grain. It was
more delicious than all other
foods. And so it was she offered
the second grain to Adam, who
had come from a walk in the
garden. At first he resisted, but
seeing Eve's delight, he ate.

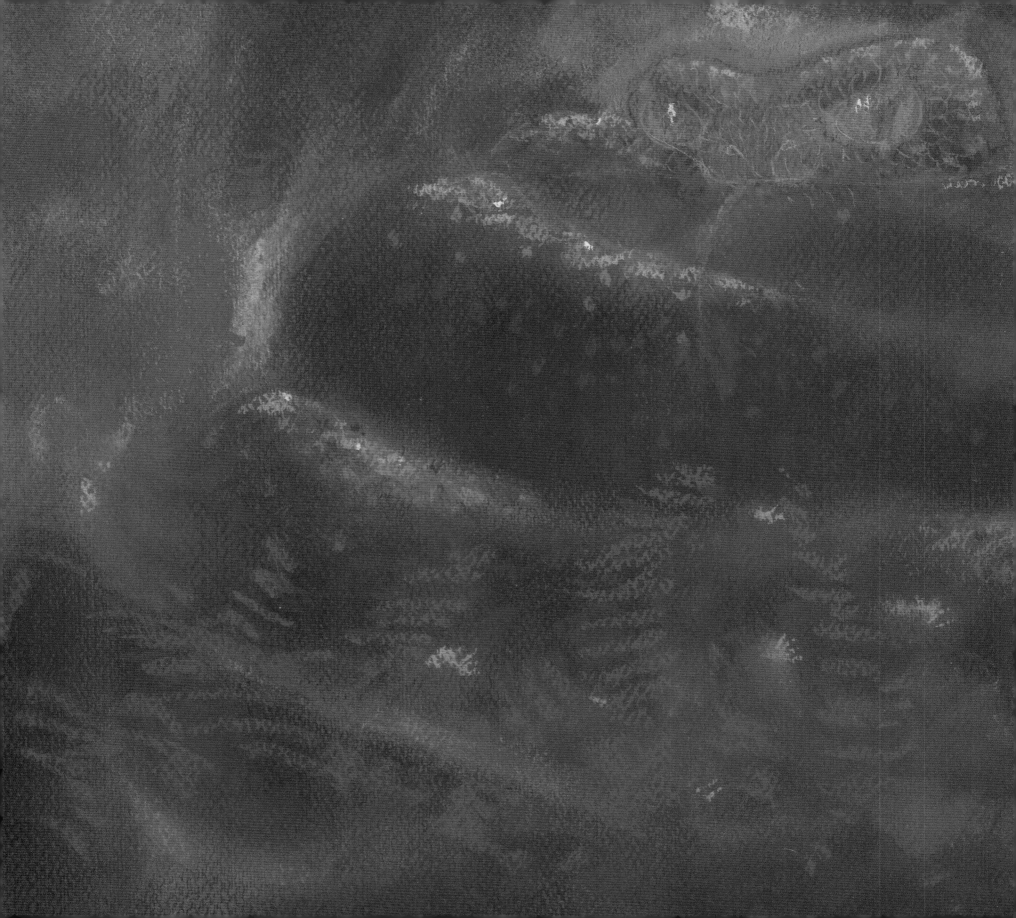

And Iblis! Seeing his evil work completed, he flew back between the serpent's teeth. The serpent coiled herself tightly, for she knew the punishment to come.

In a voice of thunder, God addressed Adam and Eve: Did I not forbid ye to touch this fruit? Did I not caution ye against the evildoings of my foe, Iblis?

What answer could Adam and Eve give? They tried to flee God's wrath, but the tree caught Adam, and Eve's hair became entangled in the branches.

God spoke again: Depart from Paradise, thou Adam, thy wife, Eve, and the animals that led ye into disobeying my command. By the sweat of thy brow shalt thou find food. Eve shall bring forth children in pain. The peacock shall lose his melodious voice, and the serpent shall lose her feet. Darkness shall be her den, and dust shall be her food. As for Iblis, Iblis shall be cast back into the torments of all eternity.

One leaf each was given to Eve and Adam to cover their nakedness. Adam was expelled from Paradise through the gate of Repentance that he would never forget how Paradise might be regained. Eve was expelled through the gate of Grace. The serpent and the peacock were exiled through the gate of Wrath. And Iblis was hurled out through the gate of Damnation.

Adam fell to the island of Serendib, which is now Sri Lanka. Eve fell to Jeddah; the serpent fell into the desert of the Sahara; and the peacock fell into Persia.

And Iblis fell into the River Eila, which flows into Hell.